Tom could not bear to thin coal tubs in the evil stinking underground. Never to see gallop over the soft turf! He knew now that he c never be a miner. He had to go ho to the cold wind and the crashing sea

Bu . . . "I must say goodbye to Storm."

A cap g and moving pony tale, by a best-sell nd award-winning author.

YOUNG CORGI BOOKS

Young Corgi books are perfect when you are looking for great books to read on your own. They are full of exciting stories and entertaining pictures. There are funny books, scary books, spine-tingling stories and mysterious ones. Whatever your interests you'll find something in Young Corgi to suit you, from ponies to football, from families and friends to ghosts. The books are written by some of the most famous and popular of today's children's authors, and by some of the best new talents, too.

Whether you read one chapter a night, or devour the whole book in one sitting, you'll love Young Corgi Books. The more you read, the more you'll want to read!

Other Young Corgi Books to get your teeth into:
THE SCRUFFY PONY by K. M. Peyton
THE PARADISE PONY by K. M. Peyton
THE PHANTOM PONY by Peter Clover
STORM PONY by Peter Clover
MIDNIGHT PONY by Elizabeth Dale

PONY IN
THE DARK

To the librarians of William de Ferrers —
to thank them for their help and kindness

PONY IN THE DARK
A YOUNG CORGI BOOK : 0 552 54745X

PRINTING HISTORY
Young Corgi edition published 2001

1 3 5 7 9 10 8 6 4 2

Set in 15/19pt Bembo Schoolbook

Young Corgi Books are published by Transworld Publishers,
61–63 Uxbridge Road, London W5 5SA,
a division of The Random House Group Ltd,
in Australia by Random House Australia (Pty) Ltd,
20 Alfred Street, Milsons Point, Sydney, NSW 2061, Australia,
in New Zealand by Random House New Zealand Ltd,
18 Poland Road, Glenfield, Auckland 10, New Zealand
and in South Africa by Random House (Pty) Ltd,
Endulini, 5a Jubilee Road, Parktown 2193, South Africa

Printed and bound in Great Britain by
Cox & Wyman Ltd, Reading, Berkshire.

Pony in the Dark

K. M. PEYTON

ILLUSTRATED BY ROBIN LAWRIE

YOUNG CORGI

Chapter One

It was a bad night. March — but no sign of spring in the gale that roared over the bare rocky island. Needles of sleet pierced Tom's threadbare coat as he followed his father out to the barns.

In the lantern light the small herd of Shetland ponies stirred lazily. Tom's father counted them.

"The little black mare's missing!"

Tom shivered. The little black mare was Dimple, his favourite. She was due to foal any minute.

"She'll have gone to her favourite place, to foal," he said. "Away from the others."

"Aye, she'd do that. But what a night to choose!" His father hesitated, uncertain as to whether he wanted to do anything about it.

Tom said, "I'll go. She'll be down by the shore, under the big rock. That's her place."

"Take the light then."

Tom was only eight, but strong and brave. His father trusted him. His father was bent and old before his time with the hard life of the islands. Even in summer the wind blew harshly over the treeless land. The little ponies grew thick, dark coats and thick, dark manes and tails and, however hard it blew, they turned their backs to the wind and survived. But they were valuable now, for the rich people in the south wanted to buy them. So Tom's father had built them a shed for the worst of the weather, and fed them hay to keep them fat and well.

"Don't be too long about it."

Tom set off down the long pasture towards the shore. He could hear the sea crashing on to the rocks and see the white spray flying against the bitter sky. Behind him the palest glimmer of light showed where the family croft lay crouched on the hillside, a lamp standing in its tiny window to guide his father back. It was that dark.

But Dimple had gone to hide, to give birth. Tom would find her by instinct. Dimple was his own, his darling, and he knew her ways. He knew her favourite hollow between two big rocks above the high water mark. The earth was stamped bare where the ponies had stood, sheltered from the sea. Tom stumbled his way towards it, the lantern swinging in his hand. The spray was salty on his lips, the wind took his breath away.

He sensed Dimple rather than saw her. The smell of her, sweet and musky together, a darker blot in the dark- ness. She was standing over something that stirred feebly on the ground, another blot, tiny, wet with both birth and weather.

"Dimple!"

Dimple whinnied to him. Tom put down the lantern and crouched beside it to see the new-born foal. He felt it over with his cold hands, but the foal was scarcely warmer than he was himself. The cold shore would snuff out its life before it was hardly begun, Tom thought.

"You are stupid, Dimple!"

But it was he who was stupid, who had not shut her up when the foaling was imminent. Because he had been playing with friends, and it had got dark, and he had thought, she won't foal tonight. But she had.

"Oh, Dimple, you've got to come home, into the barn."

He felt bad about it. He had let her down. It was his fault. The storm was not going to abate. He knew the way of these storms, how they had to roar and rage until they were tired of it, and blew themselves out. But it would be dawn before a lull came. Too late for this foal.

"We've got to go home, Dimple."

He knew she would follow as he gathered the damp, awkward little bundle into his arms. He couldn't carry the lantern as well and had to leave it. But his eyes were used to the dark now, and he knew the pony path as well as the ponies themselves. Dimple came with him, so close he could feel her warm breath on his cheek. The foal, tiny as it was, seemed to weigh a ton before he had even gone halfway. But he couldn't stop, the sleet needling his back. He was wet right through, but the struggle warmed his blood. The foal felt warm against him now, kicking with life.

"I've saved him for you, Dimple."

Tom felt rightly pleased with himself. He dumped the foal down in the far corner of the big barn on a pile of straw and stood back, panting. Dimple turned her back on the other ponies and let out a few good kicks just to warn them, and then started to lick the foal. Tom fetched some hurdles and fenced off her corner, then brought her hay and a bucket of water. The warmth of the other ponies filled the barn, and the wind roared harmlessly over the turf-thatched roof.

It was good. Tom felt as if the foal was his own.

"I'll call you Storm. That's the right name for you."

It would do for a boy or a girl. He was too tired to fetch the lantern and see it properly. The morning would do.

"Goodnight, Dimple."

But the pony was too occupied with Storm to take any more notice of him. Tom hurried back to the croft to tell his father.

Chapter Two

In the morning a watery sun shone over the sea to the east. The waves were calm now and the wind just a zephyr. Tom ran out to the barn, pulling on his jersey as he went. His father had been pleased with him and the praise sang – it was rare in Tom's hard life.

Dimple whinnied to him as usual. She was black as a black night, with no white on her at all, the only spark in her darkness the wicked gleam in her eyes. She had taut little ears which stood up over the thickness of her forelock. They turned now, to Tom's voice.

"Look at me. Look what I've done," she seemed to say, proudly, for good reason.

The foal, last night a cold wet bundle, was now a foursquare colt on strong legs, bucketing round his little run. He was quick and cheeky and black like his mother.

"Storm!" Tom called.

The colt came straight up to him, not afraid at all, butting at his arm. He was a fine colt, save for – "Why, what's this?" Tom caught him by the mane and pulled him round. On his hindquarters were two white spots, quite close together, as big as pennies.

"Oh dear, Dad won't like that!" Tom muttered.

His dad prided himself on having whole-coloured ponies. He hated what he called "bits o' white". And white *spots* — why, they were far worse than a star. That meant that his father wouldn't keep him for breeding, he would be sold. They never kept the colts, only the good fillies. All the rest were sold, always. It was their living, or part of it, such as it was. Storm would be sold when he was three years old.

Yet Tom could not help making him his favourite. He taught him tricks, how to paw for a titbit, and how to bow, with one leg bent. The colt was very strong and cheeky, a character, like Dimple. His eyes were wicked under the thick black forelock. Yet his nature was sweet, and he would never kick or bite.

16

Tom was used to the ponies going away, loaded onto an open sailing boat for the journey to the mainland, then into the hold of a big ship to go south. He dreaded the day Storm would go.

"Who will buy him?" he asked his father, in his heart fearing the worst.

"The mines, I daresay," said his father.

Tom's eyes filled with tears.

"It's cruel for a pony – the mines—"

"Aye, lad, but 'twas crueller for the women and children who did the job before the ponies."

Somehow Tom could not feel as sorry for the women and children as he did for the ponies. It was true, he knew, that down the mines the coal-tubs had been dragged from the coal-face by children as young as himself, and by old grannies desperate for a wage. But an Act of Parliament had put an end to the cruelty, and the mine-owners had turned to using ponies instead. The Shetlands, being the smallest ponies there were, were used in the darkest, smallest mine shafts. Tom knew that sometimes their backs were scraped raw against the roof, the shafts were so small.

"Men work down there too, remember," said Tom's father. He had led too hard a life to be sentimental.

"I wouldn't!"

"Nor me either. Starve, rather," said his father.

But perhaps a miner would not want his father's life either, Tom thought. The islands were cruel too. Few crops grew to sustain them, and they were nearly always hungry. The crofts were low and dark and filled with smoke from the smouldering peat fires. As well as hungry, they were often cold. Tom's ambition was to leave home and go south.

Perhaps Storm would be lucky. There was a demand for the pretty little ponies from rich ladies for their children, or to drive round their country estates in little wicker carts like Queen Victoria. And some were sent abroad to America and even as far as Australia – although Tom would not wish such a long sea journey on his dear Storm either. Some of the ponies died on the voyage. It was bad enough sailing down to Durham when the weather was rough. But there was no alternative for Storm, he had to be sold.

Tom's father would not keep him for breeding because of his two white spots.

"I don't want no spots on my ponies."

Tom pleaded with him, but to no avail.

Chapter Three

When the time came, when Storm was three, Tom begged to go with the shipload of ponies. He was eleven by then, and ready for work. His father said he could go "for a month or two" and stay with Uncle Joe, his father's brother in Durham. Uncle Joe had run away at the age of fourteen and never come back. Perhaps Tom's father thought Tom wouldn't come back either, but in his heart he wouldn't have blamed him. What was there on the bleak islands for a living, save fishing and heart-breaking farming? No comfort anywhere. The ponies were better equipped to survive than their human keepers.

When the day came, a calm day in spring, a big fishing boat came into the quay and ten ponies were manhandled aboard. It was an open sailing boat, with three fishermen to sail it. Tom jumped down with his canvas bag of belongings, and his mother and father and brothers and sisters came to wave him off. With two older brothers he didn't think he'd be missed so badly. But the ponies would miss him, especially Dimple. He had cried saying goodbye to Dimple. But her son Storm was still with him, looking pop-eyed as the big red mainsail was hoisted over his head. Tom put his arms round his neck and buried his face in the thick mane – mostly to hide more silly tears. It wasn't easy to leave home, even when you wanted to go. His parents looked small and bent and old, waving from the jetty.

The ponies were close-packed and couldn't move easily, which was just as well as the wind filled the big red sails and the boat bobbed into the Atlantic waves.

The main island was ten miles away, lying
on the horizon like a basking whale, faint
in the warm, hazy sunshine. Storm sniffed
the sea air and wondered what was
happening. He trusted humans and was
not afraid, only curious. He was used to
doing as he was told. When they reached
the shore they were unloaded and
straightaway marched up a gangplank
and into the hold of a big ship. This
was different, alien and enclosed, and
the ponies whinnied anxiously. A lot
more ponies joined them until there

were over a hundred squashed together in
the darkness.

Tom tried to see where Storm was in
the crush, but could not pick him out. But
there was a thick straw bed laid down and
the sailors said he would come to no
harm. The journey was only twenty-four
hours, not like going to America.

Tom sat on the deck with his canvas
bag, feeling as amazed as the ponies at this
strange adventure. The ship sailed into the
calm red sunset, making south for England.
What was going to happen to them all?

But the tears were over and Tom now felt only a great excitement.

The sun disappeared into the western sea and the stars came out in a great rash all over the sky. Tom went to sleep on deck, but in the hold the ponies did not sleep.

Chapter Four

The ship unloaded in Sunderland. The pony dealer met them and looked the ponies over as they milled about in the pens on the quay. Storm had wriggled his way out from the crush and stood by Tom who was leaning over the rails.

"This is a good one," Tom said to the dealer. "He deserves a good home."

But the dealer only grunted. He had some men with him who were to herd the ponies out of the town and into his fields. Tom went with them. It was in the right direction for his Uncle Joe, whose address was written on a piece of paper in his pocket.

He walked by Storm along the dusty streets. He had never seen so many people and so many horses and carts and wagons. The ponies were looking all about them with astonished eyes, and so was Tom. Tom had thought towns just had one street, in and out. This one had streets going in all directions. It seemed to take ages before the houses gave way to green fields. And what green fields! Tom had never seen lush grass like it, and great high hedges covered in white blossom full of birds singing, and trees as tall as ships' masts. Everything was so *cosy*. No bare rocks and icy spray, just soft warm breezes and green, green, green . . .

If this was the south, Tom wanted to stay.

They turned down a lane and an open gate stood before them. The ponies ran out into the big field and started grazing immediately, heads down. Even Storm was more interested in this fantastic grass than in Tom.

Tom asked the dealer, "What will happen to them?"

The dealer was a big, tough-looking man with ginger whiskers, but he had a kind heart and treated his ponies well.

"After a week or so to get them looking good after the journey, I invite the buyers to come and choose 'em," he said.

"Who are the buyers?"

"Other dealers, the mines. A few ladies and gentlemen. All sorts."

"This one," said Tom, pointing at Storm, "Will you sell him to a lady? Not to the mines. I've taught him tricks. He's for children."

The man laughed.

"We'll see. I can't say."

"He's the one with two white spots. His name is Storm."

"I'll remember."

But Tom didn't think he would.

Tom went to find his Uncle Joe, who lived not far away. His Uncle Joe was a miner and he lived not in a dark croft but in a neat house in a row with big windows and a proper fireplace with a cooking range. The fire burned coal, not peat, so bright and hot that Tom felt burned up. He was amazed by the light and the carpets and the proper furniture and the high ceilings. His Uncle Joe who was married to Auntie Bunny laughed at his surprise.

"Your dad should've left home like me! It's no life up there, no life at all."

But Tom had heard that being a miner was very hard.

Uncle Joe sighed. "Aye, that's true. You don't get owt for nowt in this life."

He described to Tom how he spent all

his working life squatting in a low, dark tunnel, chonking coal out of the wall with his pick-axe.

"No, ye canna stand up. The roof is only this high."

He held up his hand about the height of Storm's back. "And it's boiling hot down there. We don't wear a shirt, it's so hot. And the air stifles you, it's full o' dust and muck. It gives you the cough."

Tom had already noticed he coughed a lot. His Auntie Bunny sighed. "He comes home that covered with coal dust, like a black man. You wouldn't believe it."

Tom thought about it, not so sure that he would exchange the cold salt air of home for the stuffy dirt-laden air of the mine.

And what would Storm think if he became a pit pony?

"The ponies—" He faltered, "What sort of a life is it for them?"

"Same as for us, matey. Hard," said his Uncle Joe, and laughed.

"I came with my dad's ponies. They won't like going down a mine."

"No. I daresay. But they get good grub, I'll say that. You never see a thin one. And a good stable."

"Underground?"

"Aye. They don't come up. Never, some of 'em. They catch cold when they come up, you see."

Tom went to bed in a great, feather bed in a room all his own. The luxury amazed him. But the thought of the mine filled him with dread. He could not bear to think of Storm down a mine. The little pony only knew the great wide sky and the smell of the sea, the cry of the gulls, the short, tough grass. Freedom was his life. He prayed and prayed that Storm would be bought by a lady for her children.

He went up to the pony field every day. Sometimes he took Storm out on a halter, for a little walk. The dealer didn't mind. One day he took Storm up to the dealer's house, to show him how he did tricks. The dealer laughed and said, "Bring him in!" and Storm walked into the house, very polite. On the wall was a big engraving of some children in a lovely garden, playing with a pony-cart. The pony was the image of Storm. Tom showed it to Storm and said, "That's what you want, Storm. A life like that."

The dealer's wife gave Storm a bun from the table. Tom made him bow, for thank you. They all laughed.

"He's a pet one and no mistake," said the dealer's wife. The dealer was a farmer as well as a dealer, and gave Tom some jobs to do, for pocket money.

"You going to stay down here, eh? Be a miner like all the lads?"

"I don't know."

Already Tom was torn about going home. He loved the soft fields and trees and the soughing of the wind, instead of the shrieking and whistling. But he didn't want to be a miner.

Soon the ponies were put up for sale and brought into a big barnyard by the farmhouse so the buyers could look them over. Tom hung about, anxious and sick. He could tell the mine men by their pitted faces, and the hard bargains they had to drive. They wanted little ones, for the low tunnels. The littlest ones went first.

In the afternoon two ladies came in a

carriage, with a groom driving. A boy held the horses and the groom got down with them. The dealer nodded to Tom to halter Storm to show them, and another boy haltered a pretty chestnut pony with a flaxen mane and tail.

"This is the best pony," said the groom, pointing to Storm, after he had examined them. "He's very well-made. He'd make a good show pony, this one."

"Oh, but he's not as pretty as the little blonde one," said one of the ladies.

Tom said boldly, "He does tricks. Look!"

And he made Storm scrape the ground for a carrot, and made him bow to the ladies.

"Oh, how sweet!" cried the ladies.

They couldn't make up their minds. But while they were dithering, one of the mine men came up and said to the dealer, "I'll take that one. He's strongly made for the job." He nodded at Storm.

Tom cried out, "Please—!"

But the lady said, "Well, that decides it. The little chestnut one is prettier, after all. I don't really like a black. Black for the mines, that's as it should be." And she laughed.

Tom *hated* her. The tears ran down his cheeks.

But the mine man took Storm's halter without a word and led him away.

Chapter Five

"It's not the end of the world, lad," Uncle Joe said that night. "Some of these rich people's children are right cruel to their ponies. I've seen 'em."

"But they had a groom. He knew what was right. He wouldn't let him be ill-treated."

"I daresay. But lots of the miners love their ponies, you know."

But Tom could not bear to think of Storm hauling coal tubs in those evil stinking tunnels a mile underground. Never to see the sky again, or gallop over the soft turf! He knew now that he could never be a miner. He had to go home, back to the cold wind and the crashing sea.

But first . . . "I must say goodbye to Storm."

It was awful. He had hoped that Storm would be naughty and sent away, as some ponies were, to find another life. But Storm had gone to a local mine with a good horse-master. He was being broken in, and was living in a stable at the minehead. The horse-master said he was a "real good'un".

"He'll be ready to go down in a couple of weeks."

"When will he come up again? For his holidays?"

The horse-master looked doubtful.

"Maybe. But we don't bring 'em up if we can help it. Some of 'em never come up again."

The tears sprang to Tom's eyes. The horse-master saw his horror and laughed. He put a kindly hand on Tom's shoulder.

"It's not so bad, lad. They're happy enough. Warm and well-fed. D'you want to come down and have a look?"

He took Tom as far as the shaft-top, but Tom was too frightened to go down. A big cage was coming up out of a hole in the ground. It was full of men with black faces, tired and sweating. They all stumbled off and the cage rumbled back down into the black hole. Nearby the coal was coming up on a great belt. The noise of the winding machinery and the clanging and echoing of the iron gates was terrible. However would Storm understand it?

"We take 'em just to stand around here, get used to the noise, long before they go down," the horse-master said. "Bit by bit we teach 'em. No worse than working in a big city."

"Do they go down in that cage?"

"Aye. They don't like that, I admit. But it's only the once."

Tom went back to the stable and fed Storm the titbits he had brought. He hated this place! How could they work underground all their lives, in the suffocating dark, without fresh air and the sky above? Just looking down the cage pit made him shiver. And now Storm . . .

He hugged and kissed Storm, then tore himself away. When he got back to his uncle's house he said he was going home. Tomorrow! He would never come back, he couldn't bear it.

Chapter Six

Storm didn't like being shut in a stable and tied up all the time. The food they gave him was dry and strange. He had always found his own food before. But now there was no choice, just this bucket of funny stuff. But it tasted quite nice. He got used to it. He got used to all the strange harness they hung on him. And learned how to pull a wagon. They put him side by side with an old pony at first, and he had to go with him whether he liked it or not.

When he had learned to pull, he went by himself, first with an empty wagon, then with a load. They put a collar round his neck, and he learned to pull into it. Sometimes he had to pull very hard to make it move at all. But he got pats and titbits when he did it right. If he got cross and kicked out, he was hit with a stick. This was painful and gave him a great surprise.

He was not alone. Six ponies were being broken in. Some of them kicked far more than Storm, and one was sent back to the dealer for being too naughty.

"But this is a good 'un," the horse-master said. "He'll do well."

The day came when Storm was ready to go down the mine. He did not know what was in store for him. He took daylight and fresh air and the sky for granted and did not know that he wasn't going to see them again for a very long time. He was taken to the pit-head where the cage came up out of the ground. He was used to this place now, with its din, the crashing and grinding of machinery. Usually he just stood there, getting used to it, but this time

he was pushed roughly into the cage after
the men streamed out, and the gate
clanged behind him. Then the ground
dropped beneath his hooves and he was
whirling down through the darkness. He
was terrified! All his senses left him and he
shook so hard his legs nearly gave way.
Whatever was happening?

But then his insides gave a great lurch
and everything was still again. The metal
gate clanged open, and he saw dimly-lit
tunnels going in both directions ahead of
him. A boy stood there.

"Come on, littl'un."

The voice was gentle. But Storm could not move for fear. The smell and the heat were foreign to him and he had to stand to take it all in, trying to allay his fear. The boy was patient and kind. But then he pulled on his bridle and said, "Come on, we can't stand here all day." But where had the day gone?

So Storm let himself be led. The sweat gathered on his thick coat in the strange hot air. Wherever was he? He went on in the hope that somewhere ahead he would come to a field of grass and a view of the sky.

But all he came to, after a long walk, was an underground stable, a long row of stalls with lamps hanging from the ceiling to make a dim light. The stalls were occupied by ponies whose presence reassured him. They seemed unafraid and were eating happily from their mangers. The walls were whitewashed and the place was clean and the air fresher. The boy led him into an empty stall and tied him up. A feed was waiting in the manger. Storm plunged his nose into it. This was something he recognized, at least.

Maybe the worst was over.

Chapter Seven

And so Storm's life as a pit pony began.
He was put in the care of a boy called
Barney, whose job was to harness Storm
up to take empty tubs along the tunnels to
the coal-hewers. The tub wheels ran on
metal tracks, like a train. The hewers threw
the coal into the tubs and Storm pulled the
full tubs back to the pit-shaft. From there
the coal was taken by machinery up to the
ground, and Storm went back again with
the empty tubs.

The work never stopped, both men and
ponies working in shifts day and night.
Not that day or night meant anything

underground. Storm forgot that there was such a thing as daytime. He just knew feed time and rest time and work time. The work was hard, the coal tubs very heavy, and the tunnels only just big enough for the pony and tub to get through. Sometimes the roof scraped on Storm's back. Sometimes rocks fell down and blocked the rails and Barney had to heave them out of the way. Apart from Barney's feeble lamp there was no light at all, and sometimes when the lamp failed Storm had to find his way in total darkness, with Barney trusting himself to the pony's instinct.

It was very hot and Storm's heavy mane and tail were cut off and his coat clipped to make him more comfortable. Barney laughed at him and called him, "My little Ratty, my little scraped Ratty!" His proper name, Storm, was written on a board over his manger, but Barney often called him Ratty. Barney brought him titbits and sometimes a bag of grass. Storm had almost forgotten what grass tasted like. When Barney stopped for his "bait" – his little parcel of lunch and bottle of cold tea – he would share an apple with Storm and give him all his crusts of bread.

Barney had worked in the mine ever since he left school at fourteen. His father was a miner and worked hewing the coal. He crouched down under the low roof hacking away at the coal with a pick-axe and throwing it into the tub. Barney would be a coal-hewer when he was older and stronger. It was very hard work. The men

just wore shorts because it was so hot and they sweated so, and the coal-dust stuck to their sweat so that they were black all over when they finished work. Their eyes gleamed in their black faces, but they laughed and joked, and only swore when the empty tubs didn't get back in time, or the timbers that held the roof up started to creak.

Sometimes the roof fell in. Sometimes men were buried alive, and sometimes ponies too. Storm was very aware of the messages the creaking pit-poles sent as

they supported the roof, and sometimes he stopped, too scared to go on when he thought it wasn't safe. Then Barney would get frightened too, and wait with him in the sweating dark until the creaking stopped, or there was a rockfall ahead and more work to do to clear it.

Storm learned what he had to do, and would get into the right position without Barney telling him, push the ventilation doors open with his nose, back up against the tubs when they pushed on him running down the hill.

"You're a clever one," Barney told him.

Storm never kicked or bit or got stubborn.

"One of the best," said the ostler who ran the stables. So if a pony was off sick Storm would stand in for him because he was no trouble, and work a double shift. Sometimes he worked for twenty-four hours without stopping.

But he was strong and well-fed. He forgot about the sky and the fields and the smell of the Atlantic ice wind and the cries of the gulls. In his dark stinking hole he did all that was asked of him. One of the best.

Chapter Eight

Tom went back to his life on the distant
Shetland Isle, and, over the next few years,
helped his father with the farm and the
ponies. He was out in all weathers, the

wind and the rain
clawing through his
patched and ragged
clothes as he rounded
up the sheep or went
out with feed to the
little mares. He sat
in the croft at night,
trying to read by the
light of a candle stump.

Rats scuttered in the thatch. The peat cooking fire burned on the bare earth floor and smoke filled the stinking cottage. His mother stirred a big pot of porridge that would sit in the embers all night, ready for morning.

In spite of the fire, it was freezing cold.

Tom could not help remembering his Uncle Joe's house and the lovely coal fire that had blazed in a proper hearth with a chimney. There had been no smoke in the room at all. The brass fender had gleamed in the firelight and the big oil-lamp on the table had shed light enough to read easily. When it was windy thick velour curtains kept out every draught. Thick rag rugs had covered the stone flags on the floor, and pretty jugs and plates decorated the polished sideboard. How comfortable the room had been!

When Tom looked round the dark smoky hovel that was his home, he felt angry and ashamed. His father worked just as hard as his Uncle Joe. He deserved far better than this! But his Uncle Joe had worked in the mine, a mile underground, every day since he had left school. That was the way to getting a fine house with a big fire and comfortable furniture. To work down a mine.

Although Tom remembered well his feelings of horror at the thought of going down a mine, he could not help remembering more the fine house. His uncle had seemed content, in spite of his bad cough, and certainly his Auntie Bunny looked half the age of Tom's work-worn mother. She had laughed and chatted as she made bread in her fine kitchen. The smell of it baking in the oven came to Tom's nostrils again and made his mouth water. Perhaps it was worth it, being a miner?

Soon he would leave school and then there was no work save on the croft. Did he want to do that all his life? He loved the ponies but they needed little care. They looked after themselves. They wouldn't miss him. He had been scared to make friends with one again, like he had with Storm. It had hurt so much, losing Storm. He often lay awake, thinking of Storm.

When it was time to leave school, Tom asked if he could go and stay with his Uncle Joe for a couple of weeks, before he started work.

His parents knew what he was thinking.

"To be a miner?"

"No!"

He couldn't say: to think. He didn't know what he wanted. A friend of his father's had offered him a job on a fishing boat, and he knew it was a good chance. But he had seen the sea in all its moods and the idea of it frightened him. He was not very brave! To go away, just for a short while, would perhaps decide things for him.

His parents agreed and the fisherman said there was no hurry. The job would wait a week or two. So Tom set off for Sunderland again, to visit his Uncle Joe. In his heart he knew he was going to try and get news of Storm, although he knew it might do him no good. Suppose the pony was ill-used? Not all the miners were kind. And the work was terribly hard and dangerous. He might be dead by now. He remembered being told that nearly a quarter of the pit ponies were killed in accidents.

His aunt and uncle were pleased to see him again. They had no children of their own and told Tom to stay as long as he liked.

"I've got to get a job soon," Tom said. "I've got to decide what to do."

"Well, you can always get down the mine, lad, if you want to stay down here," said Joe. "But I doubt you'll find anything else, unless you're mighty lucky."

His Aunt Bunny was quiet. Then she said softly, "I wouldn't want a child of mine to go down the mine."

Joe said roughly, "Don't be daft, Bunny! It's that or starve. Would you be back north rather, in a filthy croft?"

Auntie Bunny said, "I wonder sometimes. This house belongs to the mine. What when your cough gets worse and you can't work? What then, when we're turned out of this fine house?"

Uncle Joe didn't answer.

Auntie Bunny said to Tom, "Most of the miners have sons and the mine owners expect their sons to follow them in their work. Come they're fourteen – like you, Tom – down they go, and the old people can stay in the house while the lads are working. And maybe later on when their boys are promoted, and they want to get married,

they will find the old folk a cottage somewhere to rent if they're lucky, and they can
see their days out there. It's that or the work-
house for the elderly. But we've got no boys
to go down the mine, and when Joe's finished
we'll be turned out of here. I don't think
about that if I can help it."

So it wasn't as rosy as he had thought,
Tom decided. Not much different from home
when a crofter was evicted for not paying
the rent.

He still had the choice: to go down the
mine, or go back to the fishing-boats. They
were the two most dangerous jobs in the
world, and Tom knew he wasn't brave. He
knew he had to find out more about the
mine – go down with his uncle and see what
it was like. It might not be so bad, after all. If
Storm could do it . . . perhaps he could find
Storm?

He asked his uncle about the ponies and
his uncle said the first job a boy would get
would be leading the ponies back and forth
from the coal-face.

"The boys are no good for the hewing until they're grown men."

That didn't sound too bad to Tom. Then he remembered that the tunnels to the coal-faces were only as high as a Shetland pony and as wide as the tub wheels, and it was pitch dark save for the lantern light. And sometimes the lanterns went out. And it was a mile underground. He broke out in a sweat just thinking about it.

All the same, he could not take his uncle's hospitality without working.

He asked him about Storm.

"You could ask the horse-master. He'll take you down if you want to look around the stables. You might find him there."

"Don't the ponies come up sometimes?"

"No. It's too difficult getting them up and down in the cage. They stay down unless they're sick, or there's a strike. Or some of 'em come up sometimes for a week or so if they want them for a show. That's all."

Tom's heart ached at the thought of Storm underground for ever. He *must* go down.

He must ask around for Storm
. . . unless his name had been
changed. And if he found
him – what then? Suppose
he was ill-treated? Uncle Joe
said not all the boys were kind,
it depended on the mine and the horse-keeper
how well the ponies were treated.

"But mostly the lads love their ponies," he
added, seeing Tom's face. "They depend on
'em, you see, alone in the dark just the two
of 'em."

Alone in the dark . . . that was how it was
the night Storm was born.

Uncle Joe took Tom to the mine the next
shift and – luckily for Tom – the horse-master
was above ground in his office. No, they had
no Storm in their pit. So Tom went on along
to the next pit down the road and asked
again. It wasn't a common name luckily, like
Blossom and Taffy and Billy. He did this till,
at the fifth mine, a boy said, "Yes. Barney's
pony is called Storm. Barney mostly calls
him Ratty, but his real name is Storm."

Tom felt sick with excitement. He found out what shift Barney was on, and what time he would come up, and hung around the pit-head in a fever of impatience. Each cage that came up, the men poured out, all black and shining with sweat – they all looked the same to Tom.

"Barney! I'm looking for Barney!" he appealed to the ones that looked young. "Do you know Barney?"

At last . . . "Aye, that's him." A black face nodded in the direction of another black face. Bright eyes switched to Tom.

"What is it?"

"Your pony – Ratty – Storm—" Tom could hardly get the words out in his excitement.

"Aye. What about him?"

But the boy stopped, quite friendly, and Tom blurted out his quest to see him. He told

Barney about the pony's past, how he had been born and would have died but for Tom bringing him back from the seashore. And how much he wanted to see him again.

"Well, you'll have to see him down there, for he never comes up. If you ask in the office they might let you down. My next shift's in the morning, at seven. I'll look for you."

As he walked away he turned back and said over his shoulder, "He's a real good 'un, your Storm."

Tom was so excited he scarcely slept. Excited and frightened. What was he going to prove? He guessed that seeing Storm again would only be heart-rending. Why ever had he come? Suddenly the prospect of fishing for a living had never seemed more attractive.

Auntie Bunny said, "Just you say hullo to that pony and come back up again. Sometimes, in spite of what your uncle says, I wish we'd never left the islands, Tom. You'll see what I mean."

Chapter Nine

Tom was waiting for Barney at the pit-
head the next morning. Barney was
washed and clean and looked quite
different from the shiny black figure of the
night before. He had a cheerful grin and
Tom liked him immediately. His heart
warmed. At least Storm had a kind lad.

"Do you like working down the mine?"
Tom asked.

But Barney did not seem to understand
the question. "Like? I dunno about *liking*.
It's all there is, surely?"

The moment had come. Tom followed
Barney into the iron cage with a crowd of

men, and then the floor dropped from beneath his feet and they went rattling and shuddering down and down and down – Tom thought it would never stop. Hot, stinking air engulfed him. How far down? The men were  chatting and laughing all the time. At the bottom the doors clanged open and everyone crowded out. Tom was relieved to find he was in quite a large, well-lit space, not at all frightening. Railway lines carrying tubs full of coal were being emptied onto a conveyor belt to take it up to the ground, making a terrible noise. The tubs ran quite easily on the rails and were handled by men – there was no sign of any ponies.

"This isn't so bad," thought Tom, much relieved.

The older men all walked away down the big tunnel, passing weary, blackened men coming back, but the gang of boys made off in the other direction down another wide tunnel which led to the stables. Tom felt his heart banging away with excitement at the thought of finding Storm again. He kept close to Barney, trying not to show how he felt.

The ponies lived in a long row of white-washed stalls lit by a row of lanterns hanging from the roof. It was very hot, and all the ponies Tom could see were clipped and had their manes and tails shaved off. It was hard to think of Storm without his heavy hair. No wonder he was called Ratty! But Tom recognized him by the two white spots on his shaven hind-quarters. The pony turned his head and gave a little whicker of welcome to Barney, and Tom saw the same large, bright eyes he remembered and the cheeky face. Yes, he would have recognized him, even without the spots. Without his dark, almost black coat he was a mousy grey, but not skinny. But he had scars on his back and a raw sore on his flank.

Tom squeezed up beside him and put his arms round his neck. He found that tears were coming to his eyes and he hid his face against the mousy fur of the pony's hide. He had brought carrots in his pockets and Storm nuzzled him inquisitively. He was used to titbits, Tom could see.

Barney was laughing. "The little beggar! Does he remember you?"

"It's just the carrots, I reckon," Tom said. "It's too long to remember."

He found he was laughing now, so relieved to find the pony so well. He helped Barney put the harness on Storm, including a hard helmet on his head, with just his ears sticking out, and guards over his eyes.

"We go off to work now," Barney said, leading the pony out of the stall. "I reckon you'll have to go back up."

Tom hesitated. If he wanted to work in the mine this was surely a chance to see what was involved? It wasn't at all bad so far, nothing like he'd been led to believe.

"Can I come with you? Just for this shift?"

Barney was doubtful. "Did you ask the Deputy? The boss?"

"No."

"We might catch it."

"I don't want to get you into trouble."

"No. I can say you're me brother, perhaps. With luck we won't meet 'im. He can't do owt anyway."

So Tom set off with Barney and Storm.

They walked back to where the cage came down and set off down the wide tunnel. Tubs full of coal trundled down past them, running by gravity down the very slight slope. Every so often they passed a gathering place for the tubs where they came out of side-tunnels to left and right. Ponies were pulling the tubs out of these side galleries into the main tunnel, but they were quite big ponies – Welsh cobs, Tom reckoned. Barney went on and on. The side galleries got smaller and the ponies on their tubs smaller. The main tunnel now curved a few times and the roof came down lower. Soon only one line continued, and there was scarcely room to walk together. It was getting hotter and hotter. They seemed to Tom to have walked miles. He remembered men saying the mines went out under the sea. Were they under the sea? He had to struggle to keep the fear down.

"Does it get narrower?" he asked uncertainly.

Barney laughed. "Why d'you think they use Shetlands?" he said.

At last they came to the side gallery where they were to start work. The tunnel was wider at its mouth to contain the tubs that were collected there, empty and full. Barney hitched Storm to an empty tub and set it on the rails that ran into the nearest side-tunnel. It was pitch black and so narrow that the tub filled it from side to side, and the roof came down so low Tom had to bend down.

"Keep behind me," Barney said.

Barney had a small lantern hitched to his belt. It was like a firefly bobbing, no more. Storm was walking into the pitch blackness, hauling his tub. There was no room to get round him to get to his head, only occasionally an indentation in the wall where a man could squeeze in to let a tub go past. It got hotter and hotter and the air was close and choking. Tom tried to stop the panic rising. He felt he was being smothered. The sweat ran in rivers down his back. Every so often they went through doors that opened and closed behind them. With the closing of the doors Tom felt more and more frightened, and more suffocated. Yet Barney seemed un-concerned.

Then he said, "The first time, I was right scared I can tell you."

So he must have guessed how Tom was feeling.

At one point Storm stopped dead. Barney could not get round to his head to lead him on, so just talked to him. "Aye up, lad, come on now."

Then he said to Tom, "They do that if they feel something's wrong. They know before you know."

'What's wrong?"

Tom strove to keep his voice steady.

"A roof-fall or summat like that."

They waited. Tom fought to keep down the rising panic. What was this hell – standing in pitch darkness in a hot black hole miles underground, and perhaps the roof falling in behind you, shutting you in . . .?

But in a few moment Storm walked on. The rumble of the tub wheels again was like a song.

After what seemed miles – "Aye, it's a mile and a half from the stable to here," Barney said – they came to the place where the miners were cutting the coal out of the wall and filling the tubs. Barney told Tom to keep out of the way. Here the lanterns showed a pool of light, and men hunkered down cutting at the shining black coal with pick-axes. The roof was just above their heads. It was impossible to stand upright. The flickering light showed their naked bodies shining with sweat which made white rivers in the black dust that covered them. The air was thick with dust.

"Keep out of the way now," Barney ordered. "We get stuck here if we don't make a quick turnaround."

Tom knew that the miners, and Barney too, were paid by how many tubs they could get out in a day, so any hold-ups cost them money. He crouched back in the darkness while Barney unhitched Storm from the empty tub and hitched him up to the full one that was waiting. From a sudden flare of light as a hewer turned round he saw little Storm trying to turn in the narrow space. He had to put his head down between his legs and crouch himself together, squeezing between the black walls, scraping his poor grey hide against the coal. Then it was darkness again, and the sound of the hewers swearing. The tub seemed enormous for the tiny pony.

"Come on," said Barney, and they started on the journey back.

Stumbling, crouching, sweating, Tom's only thought now was, this is no job for me! And then he thought, nor Storm either.

And he knew, besides, the danger was always there: the roof-falls, the floodings, the gas explosions. The death rate was high. The thought of being trapped . . . Tom had to concentrate to keep the panic from rising.

But Barney laughed when they came to the wide place where Storm's tub was undone and linked to the end of the long line going to the pit-head. He wasted no time turning Storm round to set off back, and said only, "You get used to it!" Tom did not volunteer to go again.

He, a grown lad now, felt the tears rising again as he made for home, thinking of the little pony, so willing and clever, doing this dreadful job. He was well-treated and had a loving lad, but the mine was a hell-hole.

"And for the men too," his Auntie Bunny said sadly when Tom told her all about it.

"But they can choose!" Tom cried. "The ponies can't!"

"Perhaps. But it's as your uncle says — you choose the mine or you choose to starve. There's no alternative round here."

But Tom thought of the dealer, and the groom that came with the ladies the day Storm was chosen for the mines, and the boy leading the farm horses to water down the lane — there *must* be something else!

At least he had learned something — he'd rather go fishing than mining. But he would never forget Storm. Maybe it was better if he had never come, the memory was so bitter.

Chapter Ten

Tom decided to go home quickly. Being in the beautiful soft countryside filled him with longing to stay. But the price was working in the mine. Impossible! And he wanted to erase his memories of dear Storm, they made him so miserable.

His aunt and uncle begged him not to go, but his mind was made up. The longer he stayed, the worse it became.

"I wish you were our boy," Auntie Bunny said.

But in the afternoon before the day of his departure, Uncle Joe came home from his shift and said there had been an accident in the next mine – the one Tom had been down.

"A rock fall, and the water coming in. There's ten or so trapped in one of the farthest roads."

"Oh dear God!" said Auntie Bunny.

Tom immediately thought, "Storm! And Barney!"

With a lot more anxious people he went out and ran along the road towards the mine. A crowd of mostly women were milling about at the pit-head, with bleak-faced officials trying to keep them calm. Tom didn't know anyone to ask about Barney and he knew better than to enquire about a pony, but he stayed on the fringe of the crowd trying to get news. As miners poured out of the cage, a lot of the crowd dispersed, finding their men, until by evening only a few remained. The word was that the accident wasn't so bad: the water had stopped coming in and they were digging through to the trapped men.

The delay had been caused by getting a dead pony out of the road.

Tom shuddered.

Where was Barney? He hadn't come up with the miners at the end of his shift.

Dusk was falling and strong lights fell on the pit-head. It was cold, with rain in the air. Tom was filled with a terrible dread. The waiting was dreadful but he could not tear himself away. Of all the ponies down there . . . why should it be Storm? But why hadn't Barney come up? Tom couldn't stop shivering, hunched behind the knot of silent women.

All the while the coal was coming out, it never stopped. Tom heard one of the women say, "Poor little devil," and in one of the coal tubs there was no coal, but a dead pony.

Tom knew.

He watched while the tub was stopped out of the line. Some men brought a horse with a flat cart and they manhandled the body out of the tub and laid it in the cart.

Tom noticed they were quite gentle, respectful of death even in a pony. It was Storm. He knew it was.

He went over to the man at the horse's head and said in a choked voice, "Where are you taking him?"

"Up to the stables for the sick ponies, till the knacker-cart comes."

Tom went with him. The man didn't say anything and the cart-horse plodded along obediently.

"They say this 'un saved his lad's life. He stopped, like they do sometimes, and the lad was behind him. The pony backed up, but he wasn't quick enough to save himself. But if he hadn't stopped, the lad would have been killed. He'd have been right under it."

Tom tried to picture getting to the dead pony and getting him out along that stifling tunnel – and failed. Storm's hide was covered in dried blood, his skin scraped bare. When they got to the stables the man unhitched the cart-horse and led it away.

Tom was left alone with Storm's body in the cart.

Then he wept. He cried and cursed out loud and climbed up on the cart and laid his head on Storm's poor bloody side. Why ever had he come? He knew he would never forget this awful day. Dear little Storm, whose tiny body he had carried all the way from his birth under the sea-scoured rocks . . . after all his willing labour, to end like this. Maybe he should have thought of the miners still trapped underground, but Tom could only think of Storm.

After a while his tears ran out, and he lay still, knowing he must go home. His Auntie Bunny would be wondering where on earth he had got to. He was very cold now, and the stars were coming out from behind the grey clouds. He must say good-bye to Storm and forget this dreadful visit. Tomorrow he would be heading out to sea and the clean life of the islands.

But as he sat up it occurred to him that Storm felt warmer than he did. For a dead body he wasn't cold at all. Tom wriggled up his head and put his cheek close to the pony's nostrils. Was it his imagination, or did he feel a flutter of breath? He thought then that it was just wishful thinking. It wasn't possible.

He sat up and put his hand on the pony's ribcage. Was it moving? He couldn't tell.

"Storm," he whispered. And then, "Ratty, my little Ratty? Are you alive?"

He stroked the funny little bare ears. He prayed with all his being, "Please God, let him be alive!"

He lay close to him, trembling, holding the palm of his hand by the pony's nostrils. He was sure he could feel a slight warmth. Or could he?

And then, in the faint starlight, he definitely saw the pony's hind leg move. He stared and stared, holding his breath.

No, the pony was stark and dead.

But the leg had moved!

Tom hardly dared breathe, watching, waiting. He spoke rubbish to the pony, saying his name over and over. And then, after an eternity, the eye flickered and half opened.

"Storm!"

Like a madman Tom jumped down from the cart. He ran to the stables to look over the doors. Only two boxes were occupied. The ponies wore heavy woollen rugs. Tom tore them off and ran back and threw them over Storm. Then he ran back towards where a light shone in an office window.

"Come quickly! Come quickly! The pony isn't dead!"

The horse-master pulled off the rugs and put his hand on the pony's flank.

"He's not cold," he admitted, "and the blood's still running."

Tom leaned breathlessly over the cart.

"He's a good'un, this Ratty," said the horse-master. "One of the best. Poor little devil. I reckon we'd best get the veterinary master down."

He pulled the rugs back up. "You wait here."

He went off. Tom climbed back in the cart and sat by Storm's head, talking to him softly. He *knew* he was alive. Yet maybe he could still die, the small breath of life a last effort in defiance of his injuries. Tom rubbed the little ears gently and stroked the bloody neck. Storm would live by the strength of Tom's will, if justice had any part in it. The cold minutes ticked past and Tom shivered in the thin rain. On the breeze he could hear the hubbub at the pit-head as the emergency teams congregated. What was this pony compared to the miners trapped below in that dreadful place, fathers of children and loving husbands? Yet Tom's whole being concentrated on Storm. Live! Live! Live!

Sometime later he heard the sharp clip of hooves and a smart gig arrived. The vet, an elderly man, climbed carefully down and brought the gig-lamp to look at the stricken pony. The horse-master was with him.

"He moved, you say?"

"His hind leg moved. And his eyes opened."

The man examined the pony carefully
and said, "Yes, there's still life there. A
thread. But not for long, I daresay. Get him
in a stable, keep him warm, and if he's
alive in the morning – well, that will be a
bonus."

"We'll need some men," said the horse-
master.

"Get them up here. There's enough
gawping at the pit-head. Give 'em something to do."

"I'll stay with him," Tom said.

"Are you his lad? Were you in the accident?"

"No. No – I was there when he was born. I know him. My father bred him."

The man nodded. He went to the gig and scrabbled in a bag and came back with a bottle. He stuck the neck in the corner of Storm's mouth and dribbled the liquid in.

"I'll come back in the morning, boy, and see if he's still alive. Keep him warm."

"Yes, sir."

He drove away. The horse-master came back with four men, and Storm was lifted into a stable and laid in thick straw. Tom told him that he would stay with Storm, and the horse-master gave him a rug to wrap himself in and brought him a mug of tea from his office. He left him a lantern.

As he turned to go, he laid a hand on Tom's shoulder and said softly, "Don't be too hopeful, laddie. It's the shock as kills them, not so much the injuries."

He departed. As his footsteps faded away,

Tom wrapped himself in the rug and lay down beside Storm. Since that first movement there had been no more. A thread of life, the vet had said. How faint, this thread – a gossamer thread? Tom settled against the still heap in the straw and lay his head against the poor scraped neck. If willing had any power, Storm would live.

The faraway noises from the pit-head were faint, and more immediate were the scutterings of mice in the straw, and an owl hooting in a tree outside. Out here, past the pit, were the green fields and heavy-topped elms, the lane edges full of primroses. At least, if he lived, Storm would have a convalescence in this paradise.

But what then? Maybe better he should die peacefully than go back in that hell-hole again. Why, why, *why* was life so cruel?

Tom, exhausted, slept.

Chapter Eleven

Tom dreamed that he was being suffocated in the mine. The terrible little passage had closed in, pressing all the air away, and the roof had fallen on his head. He threshed about and found that his arm was trapped. In his sleep he felt the panic taking hold, and he shouted out loud. And woke up.

He couldn't move. He was being squashed flat, yet the nightmare was over. He could see daylight and hear voices outside. Then it came to him – "Storm!"

The pony was lying on him. He had moved! Ouch! A shod hoof caught Tom smartly in the back. Storm was struggling to get up.

"Storm! Ratty! Be careful! Oh, thank God! Storm, you're alive!"

It was a miracle! As Tom struggled to his feet, shedding his rug and scattering straw, he found Storm sitting half up on his haunches, looking like a circus pony. Or more like a skinned rat, his namesake, his almost hairless coat oozing blood from a myriad of cuts. No wonder, if they had dragged him for dead all that way out to the shaft! Tom flung his arms round the pony and covered him with kisses. Storm gave a little snort and fumbled again with his back legs, trying to stand. He was so small Tom was able to help him, lifting his skinny little backside.

"Come on, you little beggar! Up you come!"

Ponies were better on their feet, he knew. His heart was pounding with joy. Storm's eyes were bright and he seemed to be unaware of his injuries, more interested in his strange surroundings and the sunshine that was starting to creep into the stable.

Tom remembered that he hadn't seen day-light for three years. Maybe he was blind!

"Why, bless me – the little chap's still alive!"

The horse-master was looking over the door. "That's something I didn't expect."

"Is he blind?" Tom asked anxiously.

"I shouldn't think so. It takes 'em a day or two to get used to daylight. You think at first they are, but after a bit they come right."

He came into the stable and looked Storm over carefully. "These cuts need cleaning. Gentle, like. I'll get some warm water."

To Tom's joy he seemed to think Storm was Tom's department, giving Tom the job.

"Don't let him get cold. Just get the worst cleaned, the rest can wait. He's still shocked. He needs rest and warmth. And a nice gruel. I'll go and fix him a feed."

Tom wanted to laugh and sing. He couldn't believe his luck. The little pony, so strong, so determined to live, after that terrible accident . . . He chattered to him as he sponged the worst of the wounds. The water was black in no time. Three buckets full, then the horse-master came with a bucket of bran mash and they wrapped him up again in a clean rug and watched as he plunged his muzzle into the feed.

"Tough as old boots, these little island ponies," the horse-master said.

Tom told him about the night of Storm's

birth. Then, hesitantly, "Will he have to go back, when he's better?"

"I don't know about that. Mostly they don't, after a bad do. They don't forget, you see. It can make them difficult."

"Please – try and keep him out!"

The horse-master laughed. "Have to wait and see. I reckon young Barney'll want him back."

"But he saved Barney's life!"

"Aye, well, I reckon Barney'll love him more than ever!"

If he loved him, Tom thought, he would want him out of the mine for ever.

"Trouble is, he's a real good 'un."

What a reward for being a good 'un!

After he saw that the pony was feeding and comfortable, Tom realised that his Aunt Bunny would be wondering where on earth he had got to. And he was hungry too!

"I'll come back, Storm, don't worry. I'm looking after you."

Chapter Twelve

The talk was all of the accident; the whole neighbourhood lay under an uneasy pall of anxiety. Two of the miners were killed; three others were still trapped. Aunt Bunny told Tom it happened "often enough".

"You live in dread," she said, "thinking it might be one of yours. Thank God I've no child down the pit. Soon it will be over for us, when your uncle retires."

She was pleased for Tom and his little pony, glad that he was now going to stay longer to see the pony into convalescence.

After a big breakfast and two large mugs of tea, Tom set off back to the stables, taking a long way round through the fields to avoid the continuing clamour at the pit-head. He got back to the stables just as the veterinary master, Mr Armstrong, arrived in his gig.

"He's fine! He's eaten up!" Tom shouted.

Mr Armstrong was surprised. "Well now, he's a tough nut. I thought he wouldn't make it."

He examined Storm and pronounced him well out of danger. Then he looked at the other two ponies. One of them needed a poultice changed on his foot and Mr Armstrong said he was a brute of a pony and perhaps Tom would like to help him? Tom was only too pleased. To be looking after ponies . . . this was something he knew about.

The "brute" made the job as hard as possible. It was Tom's job to try and hold him still, which he did by twisting the pony's upper lip in a way his father had taught him. He was firm, yet gentle, using a soothing voice.

Mr Armstrong said, "You know a bit about this job."

"I was brought up with the ponies, sir."

"You can come along to the next mine
with me, if you want, and help me again —
it's a two-handed job and the horse-master
there — he's useless. Just a braggart. I could do
with you."

Tom's heart leapt at the invitation. He
jumped up in the gig, wishing he could be

a vet. This was a
job he would love to do,
working with animals all the time. But vets
were educated men and not the likes of him.

"This is a big Welsh cob. He's got a great
tear in his side that needs cleaning out
thoroughly. It's starting to fester. And he's a
great baby, very nervous."

Used to Shetlands, Tom wasn't sure about big Welsh cobs. But he wasn't going to let the vet down. His job was to hold the cob's foreleg up so that he couldn't dance about while Mr Armstrong worked on the wound, but it took all his strength and courage. The cob was so strong. Tom clung on like a limpet, aware that one crashing down of the cob's foot on his own would see him in hospital.

"That's a good lad now," Mr Armstrong crooned. Tom didn't know if it was for him or the cob. The smell of carbolic stung his

nostrils. He saw the blood and pus running down the dull coat, and the gentleness of the old man's hands, swabbing and squeezing.

"Neglect," he muttered. "All caused by neglect. A bad horse-master. You poor creature, you!"

After that was a lady's dog, in a big smart house. Tom held it while Mr Armstrong put a splint on its broken leg. Even more gentle and deft. The lady was crying too much to be of any help.

"But he'll be fine," Mr Armstrong comforted her. "He's a fine strong animal."

As they trotted back, Tom asked the question that so worried him. "Will Storm have to go back down the mine?"

"Well, he's made a surprisingly good recovery. We'll have to see how his scrapes heal up. There might be some poisoning yet."

"Can't you say he's not to go back?" Tom asked. "They take notice of you, don't they?"

Mr Armstrong laughed. "Yes. They pay for my advice, that's true. And when a pony's saved a man's life – well, they're quite soft-hearted, some of 'em."

Tom knew he couldn't go home until Storm's future was decided. He would do everything in his power to get the pony his freedom. If only he could buy him! But Mr Armstrong said that, to the mines, he was worth "a fair bit". Far more than the penniless Tom would ever be able to save. Especially as he had no job.

Auntie Bunny said, "You stay longer, lad. We love to have you around."

In a way now, he did have a job, for he fell into helping Mr Armstrong without quite knowing how it happened. Mr Armstrong came on a regular visit to Storm's stable – every day there were one or two new casualties, lameness or colic, and Tom got into a routine of doing Storm, mucking him out and feeding him, and washing down his tattered body, and then waiting to help Mr Armstrong with the others. And then they would go off in the gig together to treat the neighbourhood's ailing stock. Sheep, pigs, calves, kittens . . . Mr Armstrong was never at a loss. They called at farms high on the hill-sides, smart manor-houses and miners' kitchens. The strong gig-horse ("ex-mines," said Mr Armstrong) never seemed to get tired.

And every day Storm grew stronger and stronger. With Tom's devoted attention his wounds

all healed cleanly. His coat grew back, dark and shining, and his poor shaved dock started to sprout the beginnings of a fine new tail.

Barney came to see him and hugged him and said, "I can't wait to have him back!"

"Oh no!" Tom could not help the despair on his voice.

But Barney didn't understand. "He's fine down there, one of the best."

"It's terrible for a pony."

Barney looked puzzled. "They're treated well enough, aren't they? The horse-master says he'll be signed off fit next week."

Tom told Mr Armstrong. He tried to keep his voice calm, but the words trembled.

"It's true he's being signed off next week. He's as fit now as he ever had been," said the veterinary master.

"But—" What could he say?

Mr Armstrong looked at him kindly. "When he goes back down, are you going home?"

Tom was choked. He had been living in cloud-cuckoo-land, thinking everything was going to turn out all right. It was all going to be just as it always had been, Storm down the pit and he without a job, without a future.

"Yes," he muttered. "I've no job here. And I won't go down the mines."

"I don't blame you," Mr Armstrong said quietly.

Tom had known, after all, that it was going to end. He only went with Mr Armstrong to fill in the time while he looked after Storm. He had got to like the old man, and had been home with him a few times, helped put his gig-horse away, helped him sometimes in his little surgery where people brought dogs and cats. Mrs Armstrong gave him slices of cake.

"You're only a nipper," she said.

But he was fourteen, high time to be taking money home to his mum and dad.

For a last try he said to Mr Armstrong, "Are you going to let Storm go back down?" Mr Armstrong did not reply. Tom could see the question distressed him. There was no reason why Storm should not go back to his old job.

So, time had run out, and he told his aunt and uncle that he was going home. Once the decision was made he wanted to be off, to go before he had to witness the empty stable. He would say goodbye to Storm in the sick stables, and catch the first bus for Sunderland.

"Tomorrow," he said.

Mr Armstrong said, "There's a visit I want to make tomorrow, and you must come with me. Then you can go home."

"Yes, all right. One more day."

Chapter Thirteen

It was a miserable evening at home with his aunt and uncle, who were as miserable as Tom was.

"Yet there's no way I would wish you down the mine," Auntie Bunny said. "The job with the fishermen is best. You are making the right choice."

But Storm had no choice. He was going to be clipped out now his scars were all healed, and his mane and tail shaved again. Back to Ratty. He was turned out in the small field behind the stables and spent all day grazing in the sunshine. Tom could see he was markedly happier, and noticed how his big intelligent eyes no longer flinched at the brightness of the day. He was the prettiest pony in the world.

Mr Armstrong's gig rattled into the yard and Tom climbed up, trying not to look too miserable. His last day.

They trotted fast away from the mine-head and into the country lanes. The hedges were white with may blossom and the pungent smell of it filled the air. Soon the gig turned off and followed a drive that wound gently uphill between black railings and parkland. At the top was a big house set in gardens, very peaceful. Mr Armstrong pulled up outside the front door and said to Tom, "You stay here. I don't want you this time."

Tom stayed. Funny that there was no job for him, he thought. There were three or four ponies grazing behind the railings, but they looked rather poor and decrepit. Old, perhaps, thought Tom. A large dog was asleep on the front doorstep but he did not seem in any way to need a vet.

Mr Armstrong was a long time. Tom got down and talked to the gig-horse for a bit, then went and looked at the ponies. They looked like old mine ponies, scarred on their backs. He picked some grass for Herbie the gig-horse, who was very obedient about waiting, and while he was giving it him Mr Armstrong came out with a little old lady. They came across the gravel and Tom was introduced.

"This is Miss Talbot, Tom, a very old friend of mine."

She was what Tom called a nob, rather frail but not at all sour; in fact very friendly.

"Mr Armstrong has been telling me about Storm," she said. "What a good pony he is."

"Yes, ma'm." So what, he thought?

"He has persuaded me Storm deserves better than to go back down the mine."

Tom's mind leapt to attention. "Oh yes! Yes, he does!"

"Mr Armstrong thinks Storm would be just the pony to come and live here and entertain my god-children. I have lots and they come and stay and they always want to ride. But the ponies I have are too tired and old for little children. They are all rescued out of the mines. I buy them, you see, if they are deserving, and Mr Armstrong says Storm is very deserving."

Tom's head whirled. Storm to live here, in this wonderful park! With those old ponies for company, and a rich lady to look after him! He was speechless.

"I'll settle it with Mr Grey then," Miss Talbot said. "He always does as I say!"

Mr Grey was the mine-owner. Miss Talbot moved in circles Tom had no access to.

"Even if Barney—?" Tom muttered.

"Barney has no say in it," said Mr Armstrong firmly. "Whatever Miss Talbot says – that's the law."

The old lady laughed. "Bring him up when you like. I'll be waiting for him."

Tom climbed up into the gig and they drove away. He was in a dream of happiness, hardly daring to believe what had happened. He would have to say goodbye to Storm, but it would be a happy goodbye, no tears, no regrets. Lucky pony after all, in this kind paradise of grass and blossoming trees! So different from his rocky birth-place, treeless and wind-seared. Tom thought of his own future with a little shiver. The fishing-boats in that wild sea . . . at least you were nice and warm down the mine . . . and he would be able to see Storm . . . and his Auntie Bunny and Uncle Joe really wanted him to stay . . .

He heaved a big sigh. "I don't want to go home," he said heavily.

"No, nor me," said Mr Armstrong. "I've got used to your help."

"Yes, but I've got to have a job. I can't stay at my auntie's any longer without paying her. It's longer than I meant, now."

The gig was bowling down the hill

towards the mine stables, and Tom could see Storm, a tiny black dot amongst the daisies and buttercups. His last day . . .

Then Mr Armstrong said, "How about a job with me? I've got used to you helping me the last couple of weeks. I shall miss you if you go."

Tom wasn't quite sure what he meant. His heart had leapt with a jolt, but dropped again, dreading disappointment.

"I've got to earn money! I'm fourteen!"

"I'll pay you," said Mr Armstrong. "It's a

proper job I'm offering."

Tom couldn't believe it. It was something he had never thought about, never thinking that his "helping" could turn into a job. To be a vet – yes, he had dreamed that, like you dream about becoming a millionaire or travelling round the world: the impossible. But to be a vet's helper . . . well, that was what he was already. But good enough to be paid?

"You're a natural with animals. You learn very quickly. I'm getting old and you would be a great help to me. It was my wife's idea, when I told her you were leaving. You could live with your auntie and uncle and come to me every day."

And now Tom thought his world had exploded! Not just a good home for Storm, but for him too! He was too choked to reply.

"Don't you fancy the idea?" Mr Armstrong asked. "Maybe you want to go home?"

"Oh no! Yes! Yes, I want to – to work for you!"

And as the gig bowled down into the mine stableyard, Storm came cantering over to the fence and whinnied a welcome.

THE END

ABOUT THE AUTHOR

'There are very few born story-tellers. K.M. Peyton
is one of them' *The Times*

Kathleen Peyton's first book was published while she
was still at school. Since then she has written over
thirty novels.

She is probably best known for *Flambards* which, with
its sequels *The Edge of the Cloud* and *Flambards in
Summer*, was made into a 13-part serial by Yorkshire
Television in 1979. *The Edge of the Cloud* won the
Carnegie Medal in 1969 and the *Flambards* trilogy
won the Guardian Award in 1970.

A lifetime horse-lover, Kathleen Peyton is the author
of a number of horsey titles published by Transworld,
including *The Scruffy Pony* and *The Paradise Pony* for
the Young Corgi list. She lives in Essex.

THE PARADISE PONY

K. M. Peyton

Illustrated by Robin Lawrie

"I'm Cobweb. I lived here once…"

Lauren and Tashy love their ponies, Humpfrey and Monkey, even if – as rescue ponies – they aren't really very *good* at anything. Secretly, both girls would love to be able to win rosettes.

Then Cobweb appears – a beautiful, silvery, ghost pony from Paradise. And when Cobweb joins the girls on a ride out, some of her magic seems to rub off on to their real ponies and Humpfrey and Monkey can jump beautifully…

A lovely fantasy tale about a truly heavenly pony.

Perfect for building reading confidence

A YOUNG CORGI
PAPERBACK ORIGINAL

ISBN 0 552 54649 6

THE SCRUFFY PONY

K. M. Peyton

Illustrated by Robin Lawrie

*Large anxious eyes gazed at
her from beneath the matted forelock.
"Please feed me," they said. Please!*

Carrie is heartbroken when her dad loses a
lot of money and her beloved pony, Red
Robin, has to be sold. She will *never* have a
pony as good as Robin again. And the new
pony her parents get her is *horrid*. He is a
thin, neglected, dirty pony and Carrie wants
nothing to do with him. But the scruffy little
pony really needs Carrie – needs someone to
care for him, and to love him...

A captivating pony tale from an
award–winning author.

Perfect for building reading confidence

A YOUNG CORGI
PAPERBACK ORIGINAL

ISBN 0 552 54622 4

All Transworld titles can be bought or ordered from all good bookshops or are available by post from:

Bookpost
PO Box 29
Douglas
Isle Of Man IM99 1BQ

Tel : +44(0)1624 836000
Fax : +44(0)1624 837033
Internet http://www.bookpost.co.uk
or e-mail: bookshop@enterprise.net

Free postage and packing in the UK.
Overseas customers: allow £1 per book (paperbacks) and £3 per book (hardbacks).